To David and to Lucy
with love

First Aladdin Paperbacks edition June 1996
Copyright © 1991 by Simon James
Aladdin Paperbacks
An imprint of Simon & Schuster
Children's Publishing Division
1230 Avenue of the Americas
New York, NY 10020
Also available in a Margaret K. McElderry Books edition

First published by Walker Books, London

Printed in Hong Kong / China by South China Printing Company (1988) Ltd.
10 9 8 7 6

The Library of Congress has cataloged the hardcover edition:
James, Simon.
Dear Mr. Blueberry / by Simon James.
Published New York : M.K. McElderry Books: Maxwell Macmillan International Pub. Group, 1991.
1st U.S. ed.
ISBN 0-689-50529-9
1 v. (unpaged) : col. ill. ; 22 x 23 cm.
Summary: A young girl and her teacher correspond about the whale she has discovered in her pond.
1. Whales—Fiction. 2. Letters—Fiction. I. Title. II. Dear Mister Blueberry.
PZ7.J1544 De 1991 90-50815

ISBN 0-689-80768-6 (Aladdin pbk.)

Dear Mr. Blueberry

SIMON JAMES

Aladdin Paperbacks

Dear Mr. Blueberry,
  I love whales very much and
I think I saw one in my pond
today. Please send me some
information on whales, as
I think he might be hurt.

Love
Emily

Dear Emily,
  Here are some details about whales. I don't think you'll find it was a whale you saw, because whales don't live in ponds, but in salt water.
    Yours sincerely
    Your teacher,
        Mr. Blueberry

Dear Mr. Blueberry,

    I am now putting salt into the pond every day before breakfast and last night I saw my whale smile. I think he is feeling better.

    Do you think he might be lost?

Love
Emily

Dear Emily,

   Please don't put any more salt in the pond. I'm sure your parents won't be pleased.

   I'm afraid there can't be a whale in your pond, because whales don't get lost, they always know where they are in the oceans.

   Yours sincerely,

Mr. Blueberry

Dear Mr. Blueberry,

   Tonight I am very happy because I saw my whale jump up and spurt lots of water. He looked blue.

   Does this mean he might be a blue whale?

Love
Emily

P.S. What can I feed him with?

Dear Emily,

Blue whales are blue and they eat tiny shrimplike creatures that live in the sea. However, I must tell you that a blue whale is much too big to live in your pond.

Yours sincerely,

Mr. Blueberry

P.S. Perhaps it is a blue goldfish?

Dear Mr. Blueberry,

Last night I read your letter to my whale. Afterward he let me stroke his head. It was very exciting.

I secretly took him some crunched-up cornflakes and bread crumbs. This morning I looked in the pond and they were all gone!

I think I shall call him Arthur. What do you think?

Love
Emily

Dear Emily,

I must point out to you quite forcibly now that in no way could a whale live in your pond. You may not know that whales are migratory, which means they travel great distances each day.

I am sorry to disappoint you.

Yours sincerely,

Mr. Blueberry

Dear Mr. Blueberry,

   Tonight I'm a little sad. Arthur has gone. I think your letter made sense to him and he has decided to be migratory again.

Love
Emily

Dear Emily,

   Please don't be too sad, it really was impossible for a whale to live in your pond. Perhaps when you are older you would like to sail the oceans studying and protecting whales.

   Yours sincerely,

Mr. Blueberry

Dear Mr. Blueberry,

It's been the happiest day! I went to the beach and you'll never guess, but I saw Arthur! I called to him and he smiled. I knew it was Arthur because he let me stroke his head.

I gave him some of my sandwich . . .

and then we said good-bye.
   I shouted that I loved him very
much and, I hope you don't mind,
I said you loved him, too.

Love
   Emily (and Arthur)

The End